Max Saves

Story by Annette Smith

Illustrations by Richard Hoit

www.Rigby.com
1-800-531-5015

Max liked to ride his bike.
He always went along the path,
over the grass,
and around the shed.

One day
he saw something moving
in the tall grass by the shed.

Max got off his bike
and went to look in the tall grass.

He saw a little green frog.

Max put out his hands to get it,
but the little frog jumped away.

"I will have to find the little frog before Grandpa cuts the grass today," said Max.

Then Max saw it.

The little frog had jumped
into the tall grass by the fence.

"If I go slowly, I can get it,"
Max said.

Max went slowly,
and he got the little frog.

"Grandpa!" shouted Max.
"I got a frog!
Come and see it."

Grandpa came out of the shed.

"Where did it come from?" said Max.

"Maybe it came all the way
from the big pond
in the park," said Grandpa.

"We can make a little pond here,"
said Max. "It can stay with us."

“No, Max,” said Grandpa.
“The big cat from next door
will get the frog.
It won’t be safe here.”

“Let’s take it back
to the park then,” said Max.

"Go and find your friends again, little frog," said Max.